Cambridge **Discovery Education**™

▶ **INTERACTIVE READERS**

Series editor: Bob Hastings

TRAGEDY ON THE SLOPES

W0099645

B2

Karmel Schreyer

CAMBRIDGE UNIVERSITY PRESS
Cambridge, New York, Melbourne, Madrid, Cape Town,
Singapore, São Paulo, Delhi, Mexico City

Cambridge University Press
32 Avenue of the Americas, New York, NY 10013-2473, USA

www.cambridge.org
Information on this title: www.cambridge.org/9781107621596

First published 2014

Printed in Hong Kong, China, by Golden Cup Printing Company Limited

A catalog record for this publication is available from the British Library.

Library of Congress Cataloging-in-Publication Data

Schreyer, Karmel.
  Tragedy on the slopes : level B2 / Karmel Schreyer.
     pages cm. -- (Cambridge discovery interactive readers)
  ISBN 978-1-107-62159-6 (pbk. : alk. paper)
  1. Skiing accidents. 2. English language--Textbooks for foreign speakers. 3. Readers
(Elementary) I. Title.

GV854.S35 2014
796.93--dc23

                                   2013013704

ISBN 978-1-107-62159-6

Additional resources for this publication at www.cambridge.org

Layout services, art direction, book design, and photo research: Q2ABillSMITH GROUP
Editorial services: Hyphen S.A.
Audio production: CityVox, New York
Video production: Q2ABillSMITH GROUP

Contents

Before You Read:
Get Ready!

Sometimes, even when we think we are prepared, bad things can happen. But some people turn tragedies into opportunities. You are going to read about a man who did just that.

Words to Know

Complete the sentences with the correct words.

trigger   search-and-rescue   amputate   paralympian   slope

1 Changing weather conditions usually _____ avalanches, but skiers can also cause them.

2 A _____ is a competitor at the Paralympic Games – the Olympic Games for people with disabilities.

3 If an arm or a leg is badly injured or diseased, doctors may not be able to save it. They may have to _____ it.

4 If skiers are lost or injured, an expensive _____ operation will be carried out.

5 A steep _____ can make it more dangerous to ski on a mountain.

Words to Know

Complete the sentences with the correct words.

  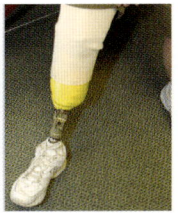  

hike   layers   prosthetic leg   powder   locator beacon

1. When snow is very light, it almost looks like _____ .
2. An important piece of safety equipment, that backcountry skiers should always carry, is the _____ .
3. After someone's leg has been amputated, they can learn to use a _____ .
4. Snow can build up in many _____ , or sheets, one on top of the other.
5. If a skier falls and is injured, someone may need to _____ down the mountain on foot to find help.

Video Quest

The Last Day

Sam and his friends were caught in an avalanche. Watch the video to see the beginning of their story. What should they have done differently?

CHAPTER 1

Happy New Year!

Sam Kavanagh and Blake Morstad were great skiers and even better friends. They met at Montana State University. In 2002, Sam earned his bachelor's degree in civil engineering, and Blake graduated in mechanical engineering. Blake was an excellent student, and was given the Gold Medal award from the Montana Society of Engineers.

After graduating, Sam went to work for the Montana Department of Transportation, while his friend Blake continued his university studies. Because Blake loved to ski, it seemed natural for him to want to learn more about snow. Understanding how snow is formed and changed by weather conditions helps to predict when **avalanches** may happen. In 2004, Blake received his Master's degree in mechanical engineering.

During these busy years, Sam and Blake always took time to enjoy the outdoors together. They both loved nature and had many adventurous hobbies. For example, Sam was a keen[1] cyclist and was on the university cycling team. He also liked to hunt and to ride horses. His friend Blake loved rock-climbing and other extreme sports. During their summer vacation, they often did these activities together while on camping trips in the rough "back country" of Montana. And of course, during the winter, they loved going skiing and camping in the mountains.

Sam and Blake were experienced skiers, and they knew about the dangers of the sport. As a safety measure, they always told friends and family where they were going. They knew that nobody should ever go skiing alone. They always brought reliable equipment. They checked the weather reports and, of course, they knew about the risk of avalanches. Blake even wrote magazine articles about avalanche awareness.

[1]**keen:** very active or interested

Late in December 2004, Sam and Blake went on a special skiing and camping trip with three old friends: Matt Schuyler, Jason Thompson, and Chris Maki. Since they had graduated from university, these five friends' lives had gone in separate directions, following different careers. Some of them were now married. In fact, Blake, who had gotten married in 2002, had some special news to share. His wife, Addie, was expecting their first child. He was also going to start a new job in Los Alamos, New Mexico.

These five friends wanted to spend some time together before Blake became a father and had to move away with his family. They were all looking forward to the chance to have fun together, like in the "good old days" of their university years. They also wanted to celebrate Blake's exciting future.

They decided to go to Nemesis Mountain, a 2,846-meter mountain in the Centennial Mountain range. It is a remote area near the border with Wyoming, not far from Yellowstone National Park. To get to their campsite, the young men first drove to a small town. From there, they traveled by snowmobile. Then they had to hike in the deep snow for several more kilometers. They had to carry all their equipment, including their skis, on their backs.

It was hard work, but these five friends were strong young men in their early twenties. Sam, Blake, Matt, Jason, and Chris were all athletes and were familiar with the location. They were experienced skiers, and two of them had certificates in emergency medical training. They thought nothing could go wrong, but if it did, they would be prepared.

During the day, the five friends skied across broad hills and snowy fields. They avoided steep slopes. It snowed a lot during this time. This added fresh layers of powdery new snow to the thick white blanket that had been waiting for them when they first arrived at Nemesis Mountain. This is what they all loved and what they had been hoping for.

At night, they partied together in their big tent, which they had reserved at the campsite. The tent was owned by an adventure camping company and was equipped with a wood-burning stove.[2] It was a simple place, but for these five friends, there was no better way to celebrate New Year's Eve. It was a night they would never forget.

[2]**stove:** equipment used to cook food and/or heat a building

The morning of New Year's Day, 2005, was the last day of their ski trip. It was a perfect day to be out on the slopes, and a perfect way to start the new year. They had discussed the possibility of avalanches, but the soft, powdery snow felt safe. They decided to continue skiing all day.

By the end of the afternoon, all the skiers were happy but quite tired. The wind had gotten stronger, but they had not noticed. They had also skied into an area where the slopes were steeper than on previous days. Finally, it was time to return to their lives and obligations[3] in the city. Someone suggested going back to the tent to start packing up. But then, at the last minute, Blake said he wanted to go for one last run.

[3]**obligation:** something a person must do, like a job

? PREDICT
What do you think is going to happen next in this story? What clues can you find in the chapter? Write them down in complete sentences.

CHAPTER 2

A Disaster Waiting to Happen

An avalanche is the sudden movement of snow down a slope, such as a hill or mountain. It is common in snowy places. An avalanche is only a **disaster** when people are killed or injured. Most avalanches happen naturally, far away from humans, so they pose[4] no danger to people. These avalanches are triggered by natural events, such as large amounts of snowfall, rainfall, rock falls, or ice falls.

Some avalanches are triggered by human activity, such as mountain climbing, skiing, snowboarding, and snowmobiling. Noise does not cause an avalanche.

Avalanches consist either of loose snow or slabs[5] of snow. The amount of water in the snow can make a big difference in an avalanche starting.

----

[4] **pose:** cause (usually a problem or difficulty)
[5] **slab:** a thick, flat piece of something

There are four main kinds of avalanches:

- wet loose snow avalanches
- dry loose snow avalanches
- wet slab avalanches
- dry slab avalanches

Slab avalanches can be further classified as either "soft slab" or "hard slab."

There are also types according to size and length. In the United States, a Class 1 avalanche is small, running down a slope less than 50 meters, whereas a Class 5 avalanche is a major event.

It is possible to avoid causing avalanches. Experts give this advice:

- never cross a slope at its middle
- try to stay along the edges of a slope
- pay attention to avalanche forecasts
- travel in groups
- carry safety equipment

Video Quest

Anatomy of an Avalanche

Watch this video to find out how the weather can make the snow dangerous and what happens to the snow when an avalanche occurs.

CHAPTER 3

Tragedy Strikes

What happened next changed the friends' lives forever. Someone screamed out "Avalanche!" Sam looked up the slope and saw a huge cloud of powdery snow moving in his direction. Sam was an experienced mountain skier and knew what to do. He raced towards the biggest tree he could see and held on tightly.

In an avalanche, the snow can move as fast as 130 kilometers an hour after only five seconds. The force of the moving snow was so strong that it pulled Sam from the tree. He became part of the avalanche, falling more than fifty meters. At some point during those terrifying moments, Sam heard a snapping[6] sound. When his body finally came to a stop, Sam knew that he was lucky to be alive. But his leg was badly injured.

[6]**snapping:** breaking, like a stick or a bone

Sam stared at the boot on his left foot. It was facing backward! He could see eight centimeters of bone sticking out of a tear in his pants. He could also see blood coming out through his pants from a forty-centimeter cut in his lower leg. Although severely injured, Sam didn't panic and managed to stay focused.

Maki, Schuyler, and Thompson had stayed out of the path of the avalanche and were not injured. They could communicate with Sam by shouting across the slope. But with a sense of horror they realized that Blake was missing. Despite the terrible pain, Sam turned his leg back to its normal position. Then he set his locator beacon to "search" and **slid** down the slope towards his friends. Meanwhile, the other men's locator beacons had helped them find Blake's backpack. Maki, Schuyler, and Thompson began to dig with their hands as quickly as they could.

Blake was buried face down in the snow. The three lifted him out and began CPR.[7] People have a 90 percent chance of surviving an avalanche if found within 15 minutes. It had already been about 10 minutes. They hoped Blake had been able to breathe under the snow. But there was no response from Blake. His neck was broken.

Maki, Schuyler, and Thompson were shocked by the loss of their friend, but they had no time to lose. They had another priority:[8] to help Sam. He was bleeding heavily and near death. It took the three uninjured friends two hours to pull Sam back to their campsite, only 360 meters away. To help stop the bleeding, they tied a sleeping bag around Sam's leg. No one knew if he would be alive in the morning.

[7]**CPR:** cardio-pulmonary resuscitation – a method to help someone start breathing again
[8]**priority:** most important task or job

The survivors needed to be rescued quickly. Unfortunately, there was no phone signal, so they had no way to call for help. In the morning, Maki and Schuyler started down the mountain. They walked through snow that was as high as their chests.

They found a search-and-rescue team, who arranged a helicopter rescue. But the weather turned bad, and the rescue was delayed until the following day. Meanwhile, a doctor went to the campsite. Sam had lost over half his blood and was in danger of kidney failure.[9] The doctor thought Sam would die before the helicopter arrived. But Sam had a strong will to live. Later, Sam said he survived those two nights by imagining himself at home with his wife.

[9]**kidney failure:** when your kidneys, the two parts in your body that remove bad things from your blood, stop working

The next day, weather conditions improved, and a helicopter rescue operation was carried out. Sam was taken to hospital, but he was still in danger. Sam's leg injury was serious and hard to treat. The leg was also badly **infected**.

Doctors were worried that the infection would spread through Sam's body and kill him. For more than a week, doctors tried their best to help Sam fight off the infection. In the end, they had a difficult decision to make. Eleven days after the tragic accident that killed Blake, doctors amputated Sam's left leg below the knee.

Video Quest

After the Avalanche

Watch this video to hear Sam discuss their decision to keep skiing that day. What resulted from that decision?

Losing a leg is difficult for anyone, but especially for someone like Sam Kavanagh. He loved, more than anything, to be outside, enjoying the freedom of sports. He loved being a part of nature. Learning to accept the limits of living as an amputee[10] would be very difficult indeed.

Sam had to learn to **cope** with his new life, while at the same time getting over Blake's death. He and his friends also had to cope with the effect of Blake's death on Blake's family and community. An investigation into the avalanche and the rescue was being carried out. The report later stated that the avalanche had been caused by Blake, who had been skiing highest on the slope. It was the beginning of a very difficult time in Sam's life.

[10]**amputee:** a person who has had an arm or leg amputated

CHAPTER 4

Life Goes On

The avalanche investigation report led to criticism[11] of Blake, Sam, and the others. Some avalanche experts stated that the friends had not been careful enough that terrible day. The campsite owner had warned Blake that the **snowpack** was unsafe. There had been avalanches in the area earlier, which indicated a risk of additional avalanches.

[11] **criticism:** complaints about

Also, when the avalanche struck, three of the skiers were on the slope at the same time, which some said proved that the skiers had not been paying attention. It was suggested that they had not tested the snow for safety. These statements were published in the media, which was upsetting for the friends. What's more, the cost of the rescue was also being debated in the community. Sam and his friends found themselves having to examine their behavior.

Life went on. Blake Samuel Morstad was born on February 5, 2005, five weeks after his father's death. Sam was depressed. His injuries were painful, and he was angry about how difficult it was for him to do things that had once been so easy. His friends tried to help him figure out what to do with his life. He returned to work as a civil engineer, but he hated his prosthetic leg and missed being an athlete.

Sam's wife suggested he try cycling again. It was a sport he enjoyed; he had cycled competitively in college. On the bicycle he found freedom once again. With his confidence growing, Sam tried skiing, too. In December 2005, less than a year after the tragedy, Sam put his prosthetic leg into ski boots for the first time. He says that, more than anything else, it was skiing that helped him recover.

Sam made a decision: he would not let the loss of his friend Blake, or his prosthetic leg, stop him from living life to the fullest. He knew that Blake would never want him to quit being an active and passionate athlete and nature lover.

Sam started cycling competitively again. In 2006, he attended a development camp for Paralympic athletes in Colorado. The coaches at the camp were impressed by his performance, and they invited him to train with the US Paralympics track cycling team. He competed in the national championships, and his results improved quickly. Sam had spent a lifetime being an athlete, and his fitness and muscle memory quickly returned. Life was good again.

By 2009, Sam was a world-class paralympian. He placed fourth and fifth in races at the IPC Track World Championships in Manchester, England. In 2010, Sam came in first in the Challenge International Stage Race in Bayonne, France, and in September 2012 he won a bronze medal at the London Paralympics for the Cycling Team Sprint!

Sam also speaks to audiences, motivating people to be the best they can be. He wants others to learn from his experience, not only to avoid danger on the slopes, but also to see that "disability" is created in the mind – not by the loss of a leg. Sam offers this message of hope and survival-of-the-spirit in memory of his friend, Blake Morstad.

? ANALYZE

Sam's life went from total tragedy to world-class success. Reread this chapter and write down Sam's thoughts and feelings, and what actions he took to make life better for himself and his loved ones.

CHAPTER 5

What Do You Think?

The men in this story were skiing when their friend lost his life. Skiing is a common sport, but it can still be dangerous, as the story shows.

There are many people who enjoy other dangerous sports. What do you think of extreme sports? Are they worth the risk?

There are already many extreme sports, and probably many more to be invented. How many of these sports have you heard of?

Extreme Sports in the Air

- hang-gliding
- bungee jumping
- ski jumping
- skydiving

Extreme Land Sports

- caving
- mountain biking
- speed skiing
- luging

Extreme Water Sports

- around-the-world yacht racing
- whitewater kayaking
- powerboat racing
- scuba diving

Even though they can be very dangerous, some of these extreme sports like ski jumping, luging, and whitewater kayaking are regular events at the Olympic Games.

Despite the safety measures taken during the Games, tragedies do occur. For example, immediately before the 2010 Vancouver Olympics, Nodar Kumaritashvili, of Georgia, died when his luge crashed during a training run. This tragic accident was due to going too fast on a poorly designed track.

Many people believe that dangerous events should be forbidden in championships. What do you think? Should people be free to participate in extreme sports despite the level of danger involved? Should extreme sports be included in international competitions like the Olympic Games?

After You Read

Choose the Correct Answers

Read the following sentences and choose Ⓐ, Ⓑ, Ⓒ, or Ⓓ.

1 Which is NOT a way to stay safe from avalanches on the slopes?

- Ⓐ pay attention to weather forecasts
- Ⓑ ski along the sides of the slope
- Ⓒ ski through the middle of the slope
- Ⓓ ski along the top of the slope

2 What did Blake Morstad study for his Master's degree?

- Ⓐ mathematics
- Ⓑ physical education
- Ⓒ literature
- Ⓓ avalanches and snow

3 Which of these does the text say is usually NOT a factor relating to avalanches?

- Ⓐ weather
- Ⓑ noise
- Ⓒ snowpack
- Ⓓ speed of skier

4 Sam and Blake lived in the United States, in the state of _____ .

- Ⓐ Wyoming
- Ⓑ Montana
- Ⓒ Georgia
- Ⓓ Idaho

5 Which injury/complication did Sam NOT have to deal with?

- Ⓐ broken leg
- Ⓑ kidney failure
- Ⓒ blood loss
- Ⓓ broken neck

6. What helped Sam the most to recover after his accident?

   Ⓐ having a baby boy

   Ⓑ skiing again

   Ⓒ going back to work

   Ⓓ cycling

7. What competitive sport does Sam do now?

   Ⓐ skiing

   Ⓑ cycling

   Ⓒ luging

   Ⓓ whitewater kayaking

8. What other activity does Sam do to help others?

   Ⓐ search-and-rescue

   Ⓑ civil engineering

   Ⓒ speaking to audiences

   Ⓓ writing books

?

ANALYZE

List three bad things that happened to Sam in the first column of the chart below. Then write what good things happened to Sam after, and how other people helped him deal with the tragedy. Then write sentences about Sam, using the information from the chart.

Tragic event	What happened to Sam?	Who helped?

Answer Key

Words to Know, page 4
1 trigger **2** paralympian **3** amputate
4 search-and-rescue **5** slope

Words to Know, page 5
1 powder **2** locator beacon **3** prosthetic leg
4 layers **5** hike

Video Quest, page 5
Suggested Answers: They should not be so "powder-hungry". They should pay closer attention to the snow conditions. They should be able to communicate with the outside world.

Predict, page 11
Answers will vary.

Video Quest, page 13
Answers will vary.

Video Quest, page 18
Answers will vary.

Analyze, page 23
Answers will vary.

Choose the Correct Answers, page 26
1 C **2** D **3** B **4** B **5** D **6** B **7** B **8** C

Analyze, page 27
Answers will vary.